Plus

CW01629609

Big Al
Jet Pee Nong Hotel
Great Prank, Frank
The Sound Of?

Publisher: Dark Novels

Please leave a review. They mean so much to authors.

Other books by Colin Devonshire

Beat The Beach - short stories featuring Thai people or Thailand.
https://books2read.com/u/mddJNE

Not Far Enough From Worries - Number 1 in No Worries series

Worry No More - Number 2 in the No Worries series

Children With No Worries - Number 3 in the No Worries series

We Have More Worries - Number 4 in No Worries series

Short story anthologies:
https://payhip.com/DarkNovels

Subscription reads:
https://reamstories.com/dark-novels

Free reads:
https://colindevonshire.substack.com/

If you enjoy my stories, there are more at
https://www.dark-novels.com
And
https://www.draft2digital.com/book/

Book seventeen will offer more short tales:

Go on get books 1, 2, 3, 4, 5, 6, 7, 8, 9, 10, 11, 12, 13, 14, 15, 16 and the others!

Keep up with Colin's twisted dark tales: www.dark-novels.com

https://reamstories.com/dark-novels

Contents

Only in Bangkok!

'THAT'S THE THING about this city; you can do anything here,' said Pope.

'Why do they call you Pope?'

'The simple answer is it's my name.'

'Yeah? I don't believe you.'

'And I'm supposed to believe Gratis is your name?'

The two men laughed and drained their beers.

'You were saying about the city?' asked Gratis.

'You can get away with a lot more here. We have a similar problem.'

'You don't know me. How can you know about my problems, if I have any?'

'Because I can read,' said Pope.

'What do you mean?'

'You are on Facebook, Twitter and LinkedIn, are you not?' Pope ordered two more bottles of Leo, 'Make sure they are cold this time,' he grinned at the scantily clad girl with the sexy bob-cut, who pretended to be embarrassed at his leer.

Bottles clinked as if friendship was sealed.

'You posted a pic of yourself, 'Plastered and pickled', did you not?' asked Pope.

'And?'

'You entered a conversation with the world, all laughing at your unhappy role as a husband in the world's playpen for bachelors,' said Pope.

'What of it?' asked Gratis.

'You want to be a free man. I have a similar wish,' Pope stared into his companion's eyes.

'What exactly are you suggesting?'

'Do you know the word mariticide or perhaps uxoricide? The look on your face tells me you are thinking of a joke. Am I correct? The words mean killing your spouse,' said Pope as he finished his beer.

'That is not a joking matter,' said Gratis.

'No, and I am not joking. I will kill your wife; you kill mine.'

The thumping hip-hop music slowed; any surrounding movement was slow-motion, the bob-cut frozen.

'Are you serious?' Gratis mouthed as life returned to normal.

'We both need to free ourselves. My plan will leave us able to get our lives back.'

'It would stop my misses whinging about not having enough cash,' said Gratis, dreaming of bliss.

'And mine kicking up about "suspected" girlfriends.'

'It was not my original idea. Other guys have got away with this scheme in fictional books,' said Pope, failing to mention the men got caught in the end.

The men shook hands, sealing the deal.

Pope explained, 'To show my determination; I will go first. When you are satisfied she's dead, it will be your turn. When we set the date, I suggest you book a few days away, somewhere plenty of folks will see you.'

The music got louder, the lights got brighter, and bob-cut got prettier. The men got drunker.

Two days later, Gratis and his wife argued, 'My mum is ill; she needs to go to the hospital,' Daeng said.

'So?' said Gratis.

'I must send her some money for the doctor.'

'Tough, I have got none.'

'You are lazy and useless,' Daeng was looking for something to throw.

He held his arm up to defend himself as his mobile beeped.

'Yeah, Pope, perfect timing,' he chuckled.

'Well now, my darling Daeng, our problems are over. I have a job interview; I'm off to Pattaya on tonight's bus.'

'*Ee, here,* you lousy bastard,' she screamed part in Thai. 'You've got no money for my sick mum, but you can afford a trip to Sin City.'

Cutlery, coffee mugs, and anything within reach rained onto the fast-ducking husband.

Gratis checked into the Sithole Hotel on the beach road two hours later. He always stayed in that place, not because it was top-class or anywhere near; he just loved the name. And they knew him.

'Back again Khun Gratis? Good to see you.'

'Yeah, I need a break from the wife,' he grinned at the night manager.

Gratis slung his shoulder bag in his room before dashing to the lively bar next door.

'You buy me a drink?' said one of the mini-skirted bar girls.

'Come on darling, sit with me,' he said as he signalled for a "lady drink", smiling all round as the "mamma san" passed over the oddly coloured little drink to her newest girl, Pinky.

Drinks flowed, and the Brit in the Arsenal shirt got louder. 'Give it a break, mate,' shouted Gratis.

'And what are you gonna do about it,' as he lunged to grab Pinky.

A half-empty Leo beer bottle crashed on the Arsenal fan's head. Stools, tables, customers and staff flew in all directions.

'You can go in the morning after you have paid for the damage,' said the police officer.

After spending a more peaceful day on a boat trip to a nearby island, Gratis nursed his cuts and bruises with a gang of youthful backpacking Dutch tourists. His last evening was spent with Pinky. His mobile beeped.

'You had better return home. The police have been hammering on your door,' chuckled Pope.

On the bus back to Bangkok, Gratis upset his neighbouring travellers as he practised his sad face, he acted a tearful display and various shows of emotions.

'Oscar, coming my way,' he laughed to himself.

He took the lift to his single-bed condo, 'Hi, Daeng, darling. I'm home. Give me a kiss.'

One stern police officer stood at the door.

'Khun Gratis, sorry, but I have bad news. Come to the station.'

Gratis looked over the brown-shirted uniform, 'What has happened? Is that blood? Oh, my God, where is Daeng?'

A message beeped, 'Now, it's your turn.'

After answering questions about his trip to Pattaya, he was allowed home, 'Very sorry, Sir, we will do everything to solve this terrible crime.'

His phone bleeped again as he reached his front door.

'What is that? Who is she? You had better be joking?'

The message continued below the photo of the fortyish European women.

'My wife,' the details, name, address and make of her car followed, 'Tomorrow at six pm'.

'But, but, she's English, that's not fair, the police and the Embassy will go mad to catch the murderer!' he screamed at the Samsung.

He answered the first bleep, 'That was not the deal.'

'Why? Because she is not Thai? What's the difference? She will meet at her school at four pm, and she will be home straight after that, make sure you are there.'

All the next day, Gratis was thinking, how? Also, how did he get caught by Pope? The police would be keener to catch the killer of a teacher at an expensive international school than a girl with a bar background.

'Pope is right; I've no connection to her or her snooty school,' the more he thought, he calmed and got on with planning.

'Plastic bag over her head? Got to be. It is quiet and easy from behind when she exits her car. That's it!' he congratulated himself. 'Oh, and don't forget to take her things; make it look like a theft.'

At four-thirty pm, a taxi dropped him at a row of shops near his target's home. He ordered a coffee and studied the surrounding area. Dressed in jeans and a Bangkok t-shirt, he looked like any tourist; the only difference was the bulge in his trouser pocket, a large and sturdy plastic bag. He walked past her address and back again. The home was a tidy-looking terrace, narrow, three floors with a garage and no sign of a dog. He clapped his hands.

A Japanese saloon pulled up at five minutes past six, and the driver lifted the garage door. Gratis leapt from behind the bins and deftly swung the bag over her head.

'Stop fighting, you silly bitch,' he squealed. This was not as easy as it looked in the movies.

Her outstretched leg crashed into the bins; Gratis struggled to keep his balance.

'Christ, you're a battler,' he sweated as she lost power and slumped to the drive. Gratis held on for a full minute as he unwrapped his hands from the plastic. He straightened, panting.

Then Gratis heard, 'Bastard!' shouted behind him, as pain ripped into him, his skull cracked as he hit the driveway, blood pooled as he died.

Pope pulled out his phone and called the emergency number.

'Police, ambulance,' he shouted. Neighbours ran to his assistance.

Two ambulances took away the bodies. The police led him gently to the station for questioning.

Later that evening, Pope made another call.

'Daeng, it's all clear. You can come to my home. We can be together at last.'

'Oh, darling…' she gushed.

She calmed herself and made one more call that evening. She didn't know the name of the person she had called, just his profession.

'I've sent half the money to your account; you'll get the rest when you complete the job.'

The END

Krasue

A PIERCING SCREAM cracked the bedroom mirror.

'Honey, what's wrong?' asked Billy, panting as his fingers searched for his wife's hand.

Khmer expletives yelled at him, none he understood. Breathing too fast, the young expectant mother regained her composure. Her chest lifted and fell gently in time with her oxygen intake.

'Where am I?' Nipa said as she looked around the bedroom.

'Babe, you are okay. We are at home, in bed, calm down. You are sweating. It must have been a nightmare,' said the shaken young husband.

He flicked the bedside lamp on.

'Christ, it is blood. What happened?' he asked.

'I, I, I can't talk…' she coughed more blood.

'Keep still. What is that?' he asked, pointing to a cord hanging from the corner of her mouth. She coughed again, this time spewing streams of red. The thread remained as if stuck deep in her stomach. The visible end swung limply.

The girl bent double, head between her knees made more difficult as the six-month-old lump was in the way.

'Let me look,' Billy said as he touched the blood-soaked shoelace like a boy tugging a worm from its muddy home.

Gently pulling, releasing its deep grip, it slid painfully up and out of her throat. Another stream of vomit soaked her husband.

'Got it!' he called, examining the item as a stamp collector sees a Penny Black.

Nipa rolled on her back and rubbed her unborn baby bump.

Billy held his prize to the light, 'It looks like uncooked bacon rind, a huge one. What the hell have you been eating?'

At seven AM, Billy left his wife to her troubled sleep in their Nong Bo Village in northern Thailand. He went to check on their livestock. Clucking and grunts accompanied him. Passing the spiky bamboo fence surrounding their property, he wondered, 'Why have we got such an ugly and useless fence?'

He quickened his pace to the chicken hut. Sensing something was wrong, he sprinted.

'Oh no,' he wailed.

His prize cockerel was gutted open, spread and pinned on the fence post. The beautiful comb has gone, along with the rest of the head.

'I loved that bird,' he cried.

The usual pleasure of Billy's morning ritual, his early inspection of their farm, drinking a mug of Nescafe, relaxing before easing into the day's work, ruined. He often daydreamed about the night he met the love of his life. Three years before, he had fallen head over heels for a gorgeous and vivacious nightclub hostess; they dated for the rest of his holiday, then returning to England, they enjoyed a long-distance romance; he proposed via Skype; she left the club; they married at her father's farm. Billy bought a farm nearby. They settled and began married life together. She became pregnant. What could be better?

'How are you feeling?' Billy asked his wife as she slumped next to him at the table, shattered. Her coffee skin was milky; the night had drained her colour.

'Yeah, a bit sleepy. At least baby slept well,' Nipa answered as she prepared rice soup for breakfast.

'Hold the breakfast; I think we should go to the doctor. We have an appointment; we don't want to be late.'

'I need to eat; I am starving,' she said, dipping sticky rice into last night's curry.

'Do you want to know the baby's sex yet?' Billy asked, excited to find out.

'It's a boy,' she answered bluntly.

Billy, puzzled by her answer, decided not to question her. That could wait. He also wanted to learn more about his and their neighbour's fences. That, too, could wait. His wife's breakfast could not. He remained in front of his laptop.

'Come on, Wi-Fi, don't let me down,' he said. Their connection was rarely reliable.

He checked Google.

'Krasue fears spikes as they get their entrails tangled!' My God, now I've heard it all,' he chuckled, not understanding the text.

Once more, he ducked the chance to query things.

'That can wait,' he said to himself.

'Good morning, have you come for your check-up?' asked the doctor's receptionist.

'Yes, we need to ask him something else,' said Nipa.

'Your appointment was booked for a scan and consultation. Is that correct?'

'I know, but we need to see him about something else too, if possible?'

The receptionist showed them in.

'Hello, no problem with junior, I trust?' said the doctor.

The doctor looked increasingly worried as they explained what had happened the night before. Changing the subject, he stated, 'The baby's heartbeat is strong. The scan is fine. You have nothing to worry about regarding the baby. I can see if it is a boy or a girl. Do you want to see?'

'It is a boy,' said Nipa.

'Yes, how are you so sure,' he asked.

Nipa just smiled.

Billy asked, 'What about the blood last night?'

'I can't see where it came from. No cuts in her mouth or throat. Any stomach pain?'

'None, doc,' answered Nipa.

'I don't suppose you kept any of the blood or the curious thread?' asked the doctor.

'No, we cleaned up and threw away the other thing,' answered Billy.

'I'll run some tests, roll up your sleeve, please,' the doctor said.

'Fantastic, a son,' said Billy as they returned to their truck.

'Yes,' said an unsmiling Nipa.

Billy studied her blank face, riveted straight ahead. He decided not to ask what was worrying her. They bumped along the track to their home.

'Hungry?' she asked solemnly.

'What is the problem? I thought you would be happy; you haven't even phoned your dad to tell him.'

'You couldn't understand,' she stormed inside, leaving her husband to check the remaining chickens.

'Your lunch is on the table; I'm going for a nap,' she called from the stairs.

Billy had eaten much of the fiery, sometimes weird North-Eastern food, but they had never served him live maggots.

'What the hell is this?'

Insulted, he stormed up the stairs.

'Don't pretend you are asleep; you've just got into bed,' he said as he shook her.

Her eyes opened wide, staring sightlessly. The baby bulge moved, rocking from side to side.

Shocked, he forgot his anger.

'What's the matter?' he yelled, touching her forehead. 'Christ, you are burning up.'

He patted his pockets, 'Where is it?' panicked, he hunted for his phone.

'Did you enjoy your lunch?' she asked brightly.

Her calmness stunned him for a minute before he could speak.

'Are you sure you are okay?' he asked again, feeling her temperature.

'Yeah, I'm fine. How long did I sleep? Better get on.'

She leapt from the bed and sauntered downstairs.

'Oh, you haven't touched your *"larb"*?'

Larb was one of her dishes he loved.

'No, it was…' he looked over her shoulder at his lunch.

'I thought you liked the way I prepared that dish?'

'I do, but it had… Never mind.'

He played with the dish without seeing maggots before pushing it to one side.

'The chicks were fine; I'll check on the pigs now,' he said, hopping out the back door.

'You wanted to know about our fences?' she asked.

'Yes, true, but how did you know?'

'If you don't like them, rip them down,' she said.

He sensed something was wrong. The pigs were unusually quiet. He quickened his pace. Speechless, he approached the mess nailed to the gatepost, once a boar, now a blood-coated carcass of rotten and stinking pork. Flies buzzed in a cloud—the prized father of dozens of piglets pinned on its back slit from throat to the anus. The guts are missing from the fetid bulk.

'Call the police; somebody has killed Arsene, our boar!'

'Don't worry, dear, these things happen,' she said, beaming.

That evening, eating on their patio, Billy decided the time was right to get some answers.

'You seem different. Have I upset you?' he asked.

'No, dear, you are perfect.'

'Is something wrong with the baby?'

'No dear, everything is fine,' answered Nipa.

'Did you mean what you said about the fence?'

She turned glaring, red in the face, 'Yes, get rid of the damn thing.'

'Um, okay,' he stammered.

Instantly her mood changed, 'Would you like some mango?' she asked sweetly.

The next morning, Billy set about ripping down the ugly, pointless fence he hated; pointless, as it does no useful purpose, but not pointless, as it offers nothing but points. He chuckled to himself, losing concentration.

'Shit, shit, shit!' screamed Billy as thorns embedded in his thigh.

Limping back to the house, Nipa hid her mouth as she beamed.

'Oh, darling, what has happened?' she asked.

'It is pretty obvious, isn't it?'

She sat him down, gently pulling the points from his leg.

'Steady, that hurts,' wailed Billy.

She smiled, putting splinters aside. She sucked on the wound loudly, like a child with her first lolly.

'What the hell are you doing?' asked Billy.

She said, 'Traditional Thai healing,' and licked her lips between slurps.

A battered Honda motorcycle rumbled up to the house. An ageing man jumped off, fuming.

'Now, what are you doing? First, you married a foreigner, and now you're removing protection for the entire village,' bellowed Nipa's ageing father in the Khmer language.

He threw his half-smoked roll-up cigarette to the ground, 'Get it fixed!'

'What did your dad want?' asked Billy. 'He didn't seem happy. Did you tell him it's a boy?'

'He was checking how the baby is and delighted the family has another male,' she lied sweetly.

The sun dipped below the horizon. Billy limped as he lit a fire and burnt the fence remains with some dried leaves he had swept up. Nipa took a mug of coffee out to him.

'Thanks, babe. Can you see the lights near our entrance?'

'Yes, it is my father and other villagers.'

'How can you see them? I only see movement and dull lights?'

'I've been eating my carrots,' she laughed.

'What do they want? Why don't they come in?'

'I'll find out,' she said as she walked the long driveway.

Billy went back to his raking. A car's horn sounded as a vehicle turned into their entrance. It stopped near the fire but kept the engine running.

'Oh, it's you, doc. Any problem?' asked Billy.

'The villagers have been calling me; they want me to talk with you about your fence.'

'Really?'

'Yes, they worry there is a Krasue nearby,' said the doctor.

'A what? I thought that was a joke.'

'Where shall I start?' queried the doctor.

'Do you want to come in, and have a drink?' asked Billy.

'Oh no, thanks. I won't be too long.'

'Okay, tell me.'

'There is a belief around these parts, not only here but also in Lao, Cambodia, throughout Thailand and into Malaysia. Usually, but not always, a female spirit leaves her body and searches for another place to live. She or it needs blood, rotting flesh or intestines to survive on,' said the doctor rushing his words.

'I read something on the web. You mean like a vampire?'

'But vampires are good-looking,' he chuckled more confidently. 'A Krasue is just head and entrails; it floats around farms and scrubland.'

'You have to be joking? How can an intelligent man like yourself believe that tosh?' asked Billy.

'I didn't say I believe it, but all these folk do. They want you to replace the spiked fence.'

'Is that what all the fuss is about? Okay, I can make another.'

'Great, that's all I wanted to hear,' the doctor stammered.

'Come in and have a beer; I'd love to learn more.'

'No, no thanks, I must go.'

The doctor dropped his phone as he clambered into his car. Driving away too fast, he clipped the hedge as he skidded past the villagers.

'I'll return his mobile tomorrow,' Billy thought. 'What was the rush?'

'Is your dad coming in?' Billy asked as his wife returned.

'No, they all have a few bottles of home-brew waiting. Talking of which, do you want a cold one?'

'Yes, join me on the patio. Let's talk about baby names.'

'Yeah, okay, do you have any ideas?'

'Not really, a couple of male names keep cropping up in my family, but they are old-fashioned. Why not have a Thai name?'

'Why not have both?' she said.

She placed a second beer in front of him, smiling and cool.

'Oh, I forgot to tell you. I was talking to the doctor and agreed to replace the fence.'

She spilt the beer, no longer calm; Nipa went to bed without a word.

Billy lifted the bottle and drained the remains. Sitting alone, he thought about his day, life, and the future.

Creeping up the stairs, he peered in at his sleeping wife. Sliding under the sheet next to her, he turned to his side. Sleep would not come. Tossing and twitching, he lay on his back, sweating. Moonlight illuminated the room.

He sensed a breath on his face.

Opening his eyes, he stammered, 'What... How...'

His ashen wife floated inches above him. Pointed teeth opened, 'Shh...'

He fell to the floor, banging his head against a cupboard.

'Quiet, I'm trying to sleep,' said Nipa.

Billy sat up, rubbed his bruise and looked around. Clambering back into bed suffered a fitful sleep.

Breakfast was quiet; Billy had questions he dared not ask, and Nipa was sluggish through lack of sleep.

The chicks and pigs were oddly quiet as he left the house.

'What? There are no eggs,' said Billy to himself as he went to the pigpen.

'Oh, no!'

They had nailed ten of their piglets to the wooden door. Slit like the boar, and their entrails dragged in the mud.

He rushed to the kitchen, 'Come quick.'

'Are they male?' she asked.

'Are what male? Do you mean pigs? I didn't look. Why?'

Nipa helped her husband clean up the small bodies and prepared them, ready to offer the meat to a local butcher.

'While we're in town, I want to see the doctor,' said Billy as they delivered the package.

'He's busy all day,' said Nipa, bagging her phone.

'Really? I'll try tomorrow,' he said.

'What's so urgent about seeing the doc?'

'Nothing much, something he said about our fence.'

'Forget the fucking fence,' she glared before turning around.

'It's unlike you to swear. What's wrong?' asked Billy.

'Nothing darling,' she said sweetly. 'Let's go home.'

'I want to know who is killing our livestock. I need you to translate for me,' said Billy.

'Why waste your, or should I say, our time? No one will tell tales on their neighbours.'

'I have got to try. I need to show them I mean business. Otherwise, we'll have no farm.'

Grunting, she nodded, 'Okay, let's go.'

As they reached the first farm, people scuttled inside the house, slamming doors and closing windows.

'It must be them; look, they are so scared. They won't even talk to us,' said Billy.

'Right, let's go home,' smiled Nipa.

'No, I'm going to the police.'

The police station was a two-man hut constructed on the main road's junction. Pulling up, Nipa stayed in her seat.

'Come on; I need you to help. I don't suppose they speak English, do you?' he said, temper rising.

Slowly, she walked to the sliding glass of the office. Two officers' feet up on the shared desk looked at them wide-eyed.

Billy opened his mouth to speak as the officers sprang from their seats and stood behind the chairs.

Puzzled, he continued in English, 'We've had problems with our neighbours. I need you guys to tell them to stop killing my animals.'

The men remained rooted and speechless. Nipa stared at them. The men looked around them, wishing they had an escape route behind them. The only door was between themselves and their visitors.

Nipa moved towards the door, and the police crouched, quaking.

'Come on. You've scared them; they must have heard about an aggressive Englishman,' laughing, she strode back to the truck.

'What was all that about? Did they think I would hurt them?' he asked, puffing out his chest.

'Yes, dear, you can intimidate sometimes?' said Nipa, grinning behind her hands.

Proudly Billy drove home expecting an end to the killings.

Back at the farm, Billy searched for tools, a saw, a hammer, and some nails.

'What are you doing,' asked Nipa.

'I'm repairing the fence I tore down.'

'I thought it was clear, I don't want the F.E.N.C.E,' she screamed.

Billy returned his tools to their chest.

'Would you like a coffee, darling,' Nipa said sweetly.

'Is the pregnancy getting too much for you?' asked Billy.

'No dear, I'm fine, enjoying thinking about our son.'

There were still no eggs for Billy to collect.

'How about an early night?' Nipa breathed.

The clock ticked to one AM. The baby moved uncomfortably for its mum. Salty moisture ran into her eyes; sweat dripped from her nose. The baby jumped inside, its tiny hands and feet searching for an escape, poking and kicking. Nipa rolled to her side, easing the pain. But not for long.

Billy slept, unaware.

On her back again, readjusting her bulge, her eyes rolled into her head; she was now gently floating above the bed.

She turned again, spinning face down, and floated a few inches above the sheets. She was now nose to nose with Billy, not touching, just there.

His eyes opened, the rest of his body frozen in place. Staring as if in a schoolboy competition, who could last longer? This was no fun game. He wet himself.

She floated lower, drifting towards the foot of the bed; his eyes followed her until she reached his groin; he could watch no longer, forcing his eyes closed. Her nose twitched. He sensed her movement, not daring to open his eyes again until her fetid breath invaded his nose. Quaking, he saw she was eye to eye with him. Hers were empty, empty of empathy, devoid of colour. Clear glass marbles watched him before floating down once more. Only a few inches this time, she slowed and stopped at his Adam's apple.

'Please be a dream,' he wished.

Her mouth opened, revealing rows of pointed teeth. He knew it was no dream as the first bite clamped his throat.

Tearing, ripping, and chewing, he was dead. She was ravenous, taking clump after clump of his throat, opening up to her goal, his intestines.

The gorge continued until sated. His stomach, intestines, and tendons had gone. She drifted into a seated position next to her husband's body.

Looking at him, she smiled and rested, knowing her task was unfinished. She waited less than a minute.

She was calm and precise, drawing a fingernail sharply across her bulge, 'You are next, my baby son.'

Opening her belly, spreading flaps of skin and fat, she lifted the boy out. She clamped her needle-like teeth down on the still attached baby, leaving only a skull and a few bones.

The Krasue floated out of the open window and swept across the gap of missing fencing.

'I told him not to fix it!' she sniggered.

Howling into the night sky, it echoed across rice fields, waking terrified farmers.

She found a new home high in a Pinus Kesiya tree. She was settling comfortably on a branch until she needed her next feast.

The END

If You Work For Big Al?

'I NEED TO see you, now!' whispered Big Al, who had a whisper that melts phones.

'On my way,' JD knew better than to argue with the man who paid his wages. He also knew that when Big Al whispered, you had better move… fast.

JD badly needed a shower, and there was no time for a shave. There was no dress code for this meeting. He slung on last night's jeans and t-shirt. Sniffing the Levis, he changed his mind and quickly found some clean light brown canvas strides and a denim shirt. Satisfied that his body odour would not insult Big Al's nostrils, he grabbed a leather jacket and drove the short distance to North London.

Big Al's busty daughter was waiting by the window.

'Go straight in. He is upstairs… Waiting,' Marilyn said, with the cheeky smile that got several men in serious trouble with her father. JD knew better than to tempt fate. He smiled and studied his trainers.

'No need to knock. Get in here,' whispered Big Al coughing cigar smoke from behind the elaborately carved door. The horse whisper was loud enough to rattle lesser men's nerves. JD heard a snigger from behind. Marilyn was signalling she wanted to talk on the phone. JD shook his head and marched in.

He remembered to sit as fast as possible. Big Al didn't enjoy guests towering over him. Big Al's sized five handmade brogues had the number seven stamped on the sole. They appeared to dance on the antique desk as he twitched his knees. His hands slammed onto bony knees as Big Al leaned forward snarling.

'You know Geordie Jenkins?'

JD was unsure if that was a question or a statement. He nodded anyway.

'He is your next task,' Big Al raised his reading glasses to eyebrow level, his hands to shoulder height, 'Don't but me,' he snarled.

'Bu… I was going to ask a question. Is Geordie home?'

'No, and he has been upsetting my plans. I want it stopped.'

'B…' JD started again, 'Last I heard, he was in Bangkok?'

'Correct. Thailand has stopped all tourism, but that is not my problem. My customers are locals, ex-pats, Thai business people and Asian gents who seem to creep under the immigration net with too much money to lose. That prat, the Geordie git, is struggling for business with no tourists. He is trying to nick my punters. So, my dear JD, I need you to stop him,' said Big Al, leaning back, his glasses slipped down his nose as the Bangkok Post headline appeared on his computer screen.

'See, the Thai government will not open their borders for the foreseeable future. I want Geordie stopped now,' Big Al whispered the words.

'How can I get to Bangkok?' whimpered JD.

'That is why I pay you so handsomely. You must complete the job. Not some unknown monkey. Get me?'

'Yes, Al. Let me work out the difficulties. I'll let you know ASAP,' said JD.

'Be here tomorrow with the details. Same time.'

'Can I come with you? I love the food and beaches in Thailand,' giggled Marilyn as JD trudged past her to his car.

The screen on his car's dashboard lit up. It was Big Al's daughter, 'Dad has gone out, why not come back so we can plan your next move from here? I've got all the encrypted passwords with details of Dad's colleagues and customers, and we can find someone to do the job there for you. You disappear for a few days, then turn up with a smile and put your hand out for your payment,' said Marilyn.

'How do you stand it?' said JD, 'I need the money, that's clear, so I must work for him, but you?'

'It's a long story, but I also have no choice,' said Marilyn as she slid a chair to JD.

An hour later, they were beaming with their choice—a French national who was more than capable of completing the task. However, there was another problem. Pierre lived next to the beach on Phuket. People weren't allowed on or off the island. This hitch was overcome by employing the services of a Micro plane pilot to drop him on the mainland. Costs of any backhanders, if either man were apprehended, were allowed for.

'Perfect,' they agreed.

'See you tomorrow at noon,' smiled JD.

JD was whistling as he rang the doorbell. Unlocked and opened to his touch.

'That's odd,' he breathed. Instantly alert, he peered around the door, suspecting an unhappy customer was paying a visit. JD then heard a whimpering upstairs.

'Marilyn, are you okay?' he called as he mounted steps three at a time.

'Join us,' was whispered from behind the door.

The stunted barrels of a sawn-off shotgun were rammed into his spine.

'On your knees,' whispered Big Al as he moved between Marilyn and JD. Big Al could now look JD in the eyes.

Marilyn strained against the slipknots which were cutting into her wrists and ankles.

'I consider myself a fair man, a generous boss and a loving father. Why do you two not respect that?' The whisper sounded like two bricks scraping together.

'We were trying to find the best way to complete your task.'

'Oh, really? You were going to use a half-wit Frog who couldn't even get off the island without you arranging it for him.' Brick dust was clouding.

Marilyn was shaking her head, 'How do you know? I disconnected all the cameras?'

'My darling, sweet, untrustworthy daughter, you only disconnected the ones you know about,' his laughter sounded like the bricks had crumbled.

JD fidgeted, which earned him a mouth full of stock. He rolled to the floor.

'It's not the "task", is it?' Marilyn breathed, 'You just don't want me to have a boyfriend, right?'

Her father stood across JD with the gun pointed at his face, 'Your mother had enough lovers for both of you,' he wheezed.

'Dad, I'm twenty-four. It is time I settled down with a husband. Like JD.'

'He works for me. He is not good enough for you.'

'But Dad, we love each other.'

'You love him, haha, so much that you'd go against your father's orders?' he snarled.

'We were getting your job completed most speedily and cost-effectively way possible with the pandemic hanging over us all.'

'God, you argue just like your Mum did.'

'I don't remember too much about her. Perhaps I should keep my trap shut? Will I vanish too?'

'You've both got one last chance. He will join a tanker leaving for Bangkok tonight. If the task gets fulfilled to my satisfaction, he can return, and I'll consider employing him full-time.'

'And?'

'And you can see him. He'd better not break your heart.'

'Oh, Dad, I love you.'

It was her turn to whisper, 'Sometimes.'

His Stanley knife sliced through her ties, and she ran to the groggy JD. Big Al went downstairs to the reception desk and made a call.

'JD will be ready for you to collect. He'll be in a golf bag, and he is packed with water and some sandwiches. Let him out when you sail. He may be groggy,' Big Al coughed. 'Easy enough to add him and the clubs to personnel belongings. Get him ashore, follow him, and ensure the task gets completed. Then my friend,' Al, looked around and whispered even quieter, 'I don't want him to return. Let's say he went out of bounds. Got it?'

Upstairs, Marilyn soundlessly replaced the receiver. She calmly picked up the weapon from the desk, checked the shotgun cartridges, and then crept down the stairs.

Big Al picked his favourite claret from the rack and moved to the kitchen to find his favourite goblet. A wide smile greeted his daughter until she aimed the gun.

'Glad you were in the kitchen. It makes it easy to clean,' she smirked.

The lorry with the shipping container arrived, and from the window, Marilyn pointed at the golf set on the drive. The driver waved and muttered, 'Lighter than I expected?'

The END

The Jet Pee Nong Hotel

'JET PEE NONG, what the hell is that?' asked the walk-in customer.

'That, my friend, is the name of a magnificent hotel in a brilliant resort on the holiday you've been dreaming of,' answered the overly keen sales agent at Rickets Travel Bureau.

'I noticed the "deal of a century" you've recently been plugging on social media. Tell me more.'

'You are in luck. We only had one spot available, and it had been booked,' said the young man with the bright yellow blazer and oversized letters RTB plastered over the breast pocket. Below the logo was a pin screaming "Jethro".

'I was in luck, but it had been booked?'

'Yes, tragedy in the customer's family. She had to cancel. So, it's yours, just give me your card, and I'll get on with booking it for you,' Jethro beamed.

Nigel Peters scratched his chin, 'I've never been to Thailand before; what's it like?'

'Oh, you'll love it. It will be hot, and the beaches will be clean, and the food is to die for… And Thai ladies are beautiful, say no more,' RTB Jethro was getting on Nigel's nerves. He considered why he was there in the first place; he needed a break.

'Okay, book it.'

'Splendid decision, Mr Peters, you fly out Wednesday from Heathrow. Have a lovely holiday.'

Nigel settled in the middle seat in the central aisle and halfway back of the Thai Airways Jumbo.

'There's always one, and he is always next to me,' Nigel mumbled as a scruffy younger man tried stuffing his over-large holdall in the crammed overhead container.

'Sorry mate, they buggered my ticket, panic all around,' he said, squeezing next to Nigel.

Pulling his jacket free from his neighbour as he sat.

'You're here now; enjoy the flight,' Nigel sneered, making it clear he wanted no further conversation.

A man was waiting at Suvarnabhumi Airport with a small sign boasting, "Mr Peter", hand-written in black marker pen.

'But I'm Peter,' an elderly man stated.

'No, sir, I meet Mr Nigel Peter,' said the mini-bus driver.

'Excuse me, are you looking for me?' asked Nigel, looking at the clipboard and seeing 'Peters'.

Nigel was directed to his seat on the bus.

The mini-bus took no time to become snarled in Bangkok's infamous traffic.

'Hello again, mate,' Nigel heard from behind.

'Yes, hi, you again. It seems we are destined to sit together.'

'Where are you going? I'm going to the beach. I deserve sand and sea after what I've been through,' said the scruffy man.

'Me too,' Nigel said, dreading the next question.

'Are you going to Hua Hin?'

'Oh, God,' Nigel breathed as he studied the overhead vinyl. 'Yes, I think that's what it's called.'

The mini-bus pulled up outside a newly painted building, "Jed Pee Nong Hotel" in foot-high letters hung above the entrance.

'Don't tell me we're both staying here?' thought Nigel.

'This way, gentlemen,' said a young receptionist, pointing to the front desk. The driver lugged the luggage to the hotel's trolly.

'Can I see your passports, please,' she smiled.

Nigel rushed his document out of his pocket, hoping to escape his travelling companion.

'Thank you, Mr Peters. And yours, Mr Jackson?' she looked as Mr Jackson searched his pockets and then his small shoulder bag.

Mr Peters was getting used to studying ceilings, planes, buses and now the fresh paint of the hotel foyer.

'No problem, sir, the police station is over the road,' she pointed, 'I'll report it missing. Here's your key.'

'Where's my key?' asked Nigel.

'Oh, we only give one key per room,' she answered.

The men looked at each other, then at her.

'What?' yelled Nigel.

'I've got you down as a couple? That's what the agent told us,' she said.

'Oh, no, I had to sit beside him on the plane and share the bus. There is no way I'm sharing a room!'

The girl busied herself with a huge ledger, 'We are full tonight, but tomorrow at lunchtime, we will have a room free?'

Mr Jackson shrugged, okay. Mr Peters did not, as they trudged to the lift.

'You have got to be kidding me!' as Nigel saw the double bed.

'Which side do you want? I prefer to sleep near the window if that's okay with you. Oh, can you keep your noise down? I need to nap,' called Mr Jackson to Nigel's fast disappearing back as he stormed back to reception.

'I am sorry, sir, but…' she started.

'Where can I get a drink?' fumed Nigel.

A folding map was handed to him, with bars and restaurants circled. Nigel marched in the sea's direction and, hopefully, cold beer.

After sampling some strong Thai beer, he chatted with a few friendly bar girls. The beers soon changed to shots of local whisky. Nigel had calmed down and was enjoying himself with one young lady. They agreed to meet up the following day.

'My God, it's gone one o'clock,' slurred Nigel as he staggered back towards his hotel.

'Can I have my key, please?' he said, proud that he didn't appear as drunk as he felt.

'The key is with... um, your friend, sir,' the receptionist from earlier reported.

'Let me in, Mr Jackson,' Nigel spoke to the door. 'Come on, hurry, I need a pee,' he asked louder.

There was no answer or sound from inside; Nigel's firmly crossed legs made it to the WC in reception.

'Have you got a spare key, please,' said a much relived Mr Peters.

'Yes, sir, I can let you in. He must be a sound sleeper.'

The room door pushed back, and the lights flicked on.

'Where is he?' asked the puzzled receptionist.
'Where are my bags? My passport!'

An instantly sober guest opened the wardrobe and then the bathroom even looked under the bed.

'Please, sir, accompany me to the police station. We must report this. At least then, you will have the bed to yourself,' smiled the girl.

No smile joined her across the road. After spending an hour with the bored night officer, a furious snarl marched back.

'Why did I have to keep repeating myself as he scribbled notes?' whined Nigel.
'His English is not so good. You were speaking too fast,' said the girl.
'So, all this is my fault?'
'No, sir, please take the hotel key and have a good night,' she offered. Thankfully her shift had ended.

A hammering woke Nigel at eight o'clock, 'Sorry, sir, but you didn't answer your room phone,' said the receptionist standing next to a police officer.

'I unplugged the phone, as I wanted a full sleep!' said Nigel as he glared at his visitors.

'Do you mind if I come in,' the officer strode to the coffee table and sat down, pulling the other chair back for Nigel.

'What now?'

'I need you to prove who you are, sir,' said the stern man in the brown uniform.

'I haven't got my passport, as you well know,' glared Nigel, pulling his wallet from the trousers he had slept in.

The police officer held out his hand, and Nigel passed the wallet over.

'No credit cards? No driving licence? No cash?'

'What? Give it here,' stormed Nigel, snatching it back.

The empty wallet hit the far wall. The receptionist's eyes widened. Her ears glowed at English terms she was unused to.

'Calm down, sir. You had better accompany me across the road,' said the officer, hand on his pistol.

Nigel slumped to his knees, head in hands, 'Christ Almighty,' he wailed as he was guided to the police station.

After a lengthy telephone conversation with the British Embassy and proving who he was, he could enjoy the rest of his stay in Thailand. A friend sent him cash via PayPal, making life easier with money in his pocket. Nigel loved Thai food, and he enjoyed watching monkeys steal fruit. He even saw a dolphin when he took an interesting boat ride as part of a trip to the nearby mountain. His guide was the young lady he met his first night. They were getting on as if they'd known each other for years.

On his third day in Hua Hin, he relaxed in a deck chair on the beach; he unfolded the Bangkok Post.

'What,' instantly, he sat up as a headline on an inside page jumped at him, like a cold fish's revenge. He felt the slap across the cheeks.

'RTB owner found dead in her home!'

For a reason only known to him, he looked around as he read, "Well-known travel agent and business owner, Mrs Eastman, was found battered to death in her bedroom. Her husband, Mr Eastman's whereabouts were unknown".

Nigel cringed behind the newspaper, suspecting Mr Eastman could watch him. He carried on reading the report aloud, "Young sales assistant, Mr Jethro Jenks, is helping police with their enquiries. Mr Eastman is known to have boarded a flight to Bangkok. We lost track of him there, said a detective heading the case," Nigel folded the paper gently on his thighs as a voice he recognised shouted from behind, 'Keep your noise down, I'm trying to nap.'

The END

Great Prank, Frank

'AND AS I was saying,' Frank droned on. Frank's brother had heard enough about how glorious life in Thailand is.

'Oh, yeah, did I tell you about Jojo's new motor-scooter? Brand new, would you believe it? We had to take it back to the dealer. And, guess what? The petrol station down the road from us has been tampering with the fuel. I wondered how they could undercut the others. Anyway, they soon fixed it. Oh, better go, I've just had a great idea. Cheers.'

Frank deep in thought slipped his mobile into his pocket as he strolled to his hobby workshop in the garden.

'Jojo, come here please,' called Frank.

'What? Frank, I'm watching TV,' his new bride answered.

'Is your brother still trying to sell that heap of junk he calls a car?'

'It is not junk, he loves that car,' snarled Jojo.

'Yeah, why is he desperate to sell it then.'

'He has had a few problems with it and can't afford to fix it.'

'I'll buy it off him if he drops the price,' said Frank.

'Yeah, really? What do you want it for?'

'We are going to prank that idiot with cheap petrol.

They struck a deal. The car crept its way to Frank's workshop. Banging and clattering upset the neighbours for days.

'Well, what do you think?' asked Frank.

'It looks the same to me,' answered Jojo.

'Good, it's supposed to.'

'Frank, what have you done, why are the seats over there?' she pointed to a pile of discarded car parts in the corner.

'Look inside, we have improved seats,' Frank grinned.

'They are metal, they don't look very comfortable?'

'No, my dear, they do not need to be comfortable,' he banged on the hollow steel. His wife shook her head.

Frank crouched and pointed under the chassis, 'Look.'

A grumbling girl looked at metal boxes all linked to the underside of the car.

'Yeah, and?' she said, thinking of her spicy lunch.

'Those are tanks too,' Frank announced proudly.

'It will be better to leave it until tomorrow,' he said.

'What are you talking about now?' asked Jojo.

'Tomorrow is April the first,' stated Frank.

'So?'

'April Fools Day, don't you Thais know anything?'

A less-than-impressed wife stalked back to her soap operas. Frank was beaming at his project.

After tutting, Jojo clicked to Channel Seven with the handsome young star.

Frank, proud of himself opened a bottle of Singha beer and daydreamed of tomorrow.

Bright and early the next morning Frank called up to the bedroom, 'Hon, splendid news for you. That burger joint you love is offering left-handed burgers. Shall we try it later? I'll have a normal one, you can try the cack-handed one.'

'Don't be so bloody stupid,' she turned over.

'It says here in the Bangkok Post and they offer a cut-price if you mention the ad. I'll see you later, I'm off to get some petrol.'

Frank slammed the door and kicked it as he got out and walked around the aged saloon, 'Start you bastard,' he screamed at the car.

After calming himself, he slid across the seat and tried turning the key again.

Cough, cough, splutter, splutter, it fired.

'Great, now the fun starts,' he rubbed his hands as the car crawled to the petrol station.

Other vehicles tooted at the slow-moving saloon, the under chassis tanks scraped on bumps in the road, Frank found it tricky to stop himself from sliding off the seat. He had stripped the indicator wiring along with all unnecessary equipment to allow for more tank space. The car turned left (without signalling), and up to the forecourt offering five-star premium petrol.

'Fill her up, shall I?' smirked the garage owner.

'Yeah, and wash the windscreen,' smiled Frank. Unlike the UK, Thailand's petrol garages offered assisted fill-ups.

With the nozzle in place, Frank slid out, 'I'm just popping to the convenience store to get some fags, won't be long,' he pointed next door.

Crouching behind the wall, he sniggered. The garage owner mopped the windscreen and noticed the seating inside.

'Foreigners are all mad,' he said, 'How can you be comfortable with those,' shaking his head as he chucked the rags into the bucket.

He glanced at the gauge's needle spinning round. Scratching his head, he wondered what his record sale was. A petrol-soaked handkerchief wiped the sweat out of his eyes.

'Bloody boiling again,' he cursed Thailand's hottest month even at that early hour. 'Still not full, how big is that tank?' he muttered.

Frank was taking photographs with his phone from his hiding spot, 'My brother will love this,' he chuckled.

The garage owner noticed a liquid seeping under the car, 'Christ, that's a lot of water coming from the air-con?'

'Oh, no,' he could smell petrol. He rushed to the nozzle.

He grabbed the handle and pull as he might it would not budge. Frank laughed as his final adaption proved to be a great success. The tanks were still filling.

Frank's phone was now taking video shots as he edged closed. A cigarette hung loosely from his mouth.

The business owner had not noticed him walking towards his car. He was pulling and twisting at the disobedient nozzle.

'Haven't you finished yet?' Frank shouted.

Fear smacked the petrol man like a police truncheon to the teeth, 'Put that cigarette out!' he wailed, the split liquid soaked his flip-flops, panic took hold of the man as he held the nozzle to stop him from toppling backwards.

'What's the matter,' Frank started speaking as the cigarette bounced loosely lip to lip before it fell. Frank moved to catch it, before quickly snatching his hands away from the heat. The glowing tobacco hit Frank's shirt front before sparking its way to the concrete.

The petrol station owner turned away like a prima ballerina, before tripping his way between pumps, past his office door and leaping into the bushes beyond hands on head.

The cigarette turned from explosive danger to damp squib; it fizzled to nothing in the puddle.

Frank struggled to control his wobbling girth as he roared. Tears of laughter splattered his scorched shirt. He bent down and turned off the water main, disconnected the water pipe from the semi-hidden petrol tube and left it hanging.

He left his car where it was. 'There was water in the petrol before, now there is petrol in the water.' He chuckled as he walked home, checking his videos. 'Enjoy bro,' he added to the comments.

The END

The Sound Of?

'WHERE AM I? What has happened?' I thought to myself. What was the last thing I could remember? She was beautiful, that was for sure, but who was she? Yes, it is coming back; we were shoeless, dancing on one of Thailand's pristine beaches, and her smile entranced me. I would follow that woman anywhere. We sat at a beachfront restaurant, and she spoon-fed me. Food I would never order myself. Christ, what was I eating? I could see children playing volleyball, kicking sand up and laughing as the ball bounced towards the sea. A fishing boat dragging a net above the waves. Was I there? Was it even me?

'Darkness, soundless, senseless. And, painless.'

'It feels as if I'm floating in the black.'

'Black, what?' I wonder.

How much later? There was no way of telling, but grey emerged from the centre of black. The grey circle grew slowly, but it got bigger. I could not stop it.

'Do I want it to stop?'

It grew, becoming less grey as if light broke the morning. I could see! A white ceiling stared down at me, motionless, shadowless. But something.

I could not speak. My mouth did not open. A shadow moved across the ceiling, then another. My head moved sideways. Everything was pristine white, a gurney, a cabinet, clean and shiny, empty shelves and a white wall. My head, once again, stared ahead at the ceiling. But what is that? A white-coated armpit stretched across my vision. Then a talking head appeared in front of me. His lips were moving, opening and closing, not chewing, speaking.

He was talking to me, asking something. His clear perspex facial shield moved aside to be replaced with another. This time a female. She was talking too. Was that her? She looked Asian, but she couldn't be that old.

She signalled with her fingers, one, two, three. I tried to nod. Maybe my eyes glinted; I don't know. As a reward, they turned me to the right.

'What is that?'

A headless body, motionless, lay relaxed. 'Where is his head,' I wondered.

Blackness swamped me.

'What happened? Was it something I did?'

The grey reappeared, spreading quicker this time. I could see it again. And I could blink, not slowly and softly, one eye as in a wink, but more mechanically, up and down, both eyes at once. At least I could see.

'What is that feeling?'

A mouse silently moving in my head, I have moved again. This time I could see a desk. On the wall was a clock, eleven-fifty-five, I noticed and a date—Twenty-first of the fourth month of the two thousand and seventy-second year.

'Christ, where have I been?'

Once more, they lost me in black. As if awakening, I looked at somebody's legs and a lithe body, not mine.

The two faces were mouthing at me again. Mouthing and pointing.

I nodded; Christ, I can nod?

They smiled. The female grabbed an iPad and scrawled a question.

'Can't you hear?'

I shook my head.

The two heads bobbed in deep conversation. They helped me to a sitting position.

I had arms and legs; they moved, and my fingers waggled under my control. I smiled. Then I felt my face. It wasn't me. Soft, rubbery, and hairless.

They were talking again, excited children on Christmas morning.

The iPad stabbed my cheek as it was thrust in my face.

'Welcome back to the world!'

'What about my ears?' I typed.

'A hitch, we are working on it,' hastily typed.

'I thought I would be hungry or thirsty after an operation?' I typed.

'No need for food or water,' she typed.

'What?'

'Look in the mirror, over there,' she pointed.

Unsteadily I wobbled from the slab, one leg in front of the other, and made my way across the room.

'No drink? No food? No sex? Can I go back to sleep?'

'No need for sleep,' she mouthed. 'But welcome to Thailand.'

The END

If you enjoy my stories, there are more at
https://www.dark-novels.com
And
https://www.draft2digital.com/book/

How did you enjoy this book?

Book seventeen will offer more short tales:

Go on get books 1, 2, 3, 4, 5, 6, 7, 8, 9, 10, 11, 12, 13, 14, 15, 16 and the others!

Keep up with Colin's twisted dark tales: www.dark-novels.com

Thank you for reading this far. Do you wish there was a way to get your hands on the latest and greatest short stories or novels without spending a fortune? If so, a fictional novels subscription service is the perfect solution!

What is a fictional novels subscription service?

A fictional stories subscription service is a monthly service that delivers new tales to your door. You can choose from various plans, each offering a different number of books per month.

How does it work?

You will be asked to create an account when you sign up for a subscription service. Once your account is created, you can browse the selection of available novels. Then, when you find a story you want to read, add it to your cart and checkout.

Benefits of a fictional novels subscription service

There are many benefits to subscribing to a book service. Here are just a few:

Convenience: You don't have to go to the bookstore or library to get your next book. It will be delivered right to your door.

Affordability: Subscription services often offer discounts on the retail price of novels.

Variety: You can choose from various novels, including new releases, bestsellers, and classic stories.

New releases: Subscription services often get new releases before they are available in stores.

No commitment: You can cancel your subscription at any time.

Conclusion

If you are a fan of fictional novels, a subscription service is the perfect way to get your hands on the latest and greatest books without spending a fortune. With a subscription service, you can enjoy the convenience, affordability, and variety of having new novels delivered right to your door.

Sign up today and start reading!

https://reamstories.com/dark-novels

Or buy the anthologies, for only £0.99 at

https://payhip.com/DarkNovels

Printed in Great Britain
by Amazon

63244731R00048